A Keepsake Memory

Copyright © Nick Voro 2024

First Edition

A Keepsake Memory

VoroBooks, Etobicoke, Ontario, Canada

ISBN: 978-1-7383199-1-6

Typesetting and additional design by Lee Thompson Editing+

To contact the author: Nick_Voro@hotmail.com

A KEEPSAKE MEMORY

I HAVE TO HAND IT TO THEM—they were efficient. In spite of my pleadings, I not only dressed but packed my suitcase and somehow quieted down long enough to follow their diplomatic order of things.

They were professional, government-sanctioned agents (or so their inner pocketed badges pronounced them to be), and I was just a civilian without their security clearance or level of expertise.

They sandwiched me once we merged with the foot traffic in the corridor outside of my hospital room, one on either side applying just enough bodily pressure for me not to forget they were there.

Not a soul gave us a passing look. That is how superbly they conducted themselves, how perfectly they blended in with their immediate environment. And honestly, I could not knock their treatment of me—just a pair of friendly chaperones transporting a teenage girl through the hospital.

This was not meant to last. Outside, in the parking lot, as we approached an unmarked white van, they tased me with devilish synchronicity. Electricity shot through me. I was weightless, seemingly suspended in midair before they put me down on the armored-plated vehicle's floor.

They instructed me to take a seat on the metal bench molded into the framework of the van and secured my left wrist to a mounted bar running the length of the van. The bracelet pinched and made a very annoying clanging noise. Doors slammed shut and someone outside tapped twice to initiate this unauthorized transfer of human cargo.

The van jolted forward; I slipped off the bench and pain swiftly soared up my imprisoned arm. When I looked down, I noticed specks of blood beginning to appear underneath the shiny metal, which must have been wiped to gleaming perfection with some skin irritating, corrosive substance. It bitterly stung my still-scabbed wrists.

Locked inside this prisoner transport vehicle, I thought about why I was being treated like a war criminal. I probably had my politically correct politician stepfather to thank for that; for teaching a valuable life lesson to his not-yet eighteen and out-of-control teenage daughter, an insignificant little girl standing before a man and a cause (not just a man—a man with a vision; a vision of a Utopia, a New Mesopotamia right on the steps of Capitol Hill).

The unseen driver applied the brake, and the van slowed noticeably. After making one more turn, it came to a halt. The twin-suited brick-armed giants made another appearance, unlocked my fashionable, blood-coated bracelet and brought me out into the light of day.

It took a moment for a city dweller, not to mention an absent-minded one like myself, to acclimatize. A reddish brick structure, a few stories high (unmistakably an abbey), greeted me. It had medieval-looking gates, a giant courtyard, and two tall towers.

The whole thing was misplaced, surrounded by nothing but desert and endless weeds covering the dry, deficient soil. I heard a door slam, the engine start up, and helplessly I watched the van speed away. No one seemed worried about me making a run for it. Why would they worry? Where could I possibly go? With only one option, one path to take, I approached this isolated abomination, made it past the walk-through chain-link fence gate, already unlocked, my arrival plainly anticipated beforehand, and found myself beneath a crimson awning shading the front doors, my hand nervously clutching the handle of the suitcase. I will not deny being awash with dread, terrified to take the first step toward my rehabilitation.

Thankfully, Dr. Brown was there to help me along, a tradesman of commodities, such as favors. You do him one and he does you one back. All he asked of me was to come inside and, in return... well, that I never got to find out. They discovered his partly vermin-mutilated corpse face down in the boiler room three days after I made my miraculous escape and finally got around to phoning in the anonymous tip off.

Once the information was out there, newspapers wasted no time clashing, simultaneously reporting this headliner story:

"Asylum Scandal: One man found dead, presumed to be a doctor, in the boiler room of an abandoned abbey clandestinely converted into an operational medical facility, laying face down with two bullet holes in the back of his head, an execution-style murder according to the detectives assigned to the case. The man's colleague, attired similarly in a white doctor's lab coat, was located upstairs, bloody but alive, crudely tied to a patient's bed and refusing to cooperate with the police, stonewalling the entire active investigation. Foul play is very much suspected. Stay tuned for more information about this broadening scandal."

They handled it very professionally and tastefully I must say, I would have titled it, "Asylum Scandal, or What's a Ph.D. to a Rat," with the first line going something like this, "Boiler room rats have a banquet… dismembering, mutilating and gnawing on a celebrated doctor in the field of…" But this is me acting my own age, showing that bit of immaturity almost expected of me. Newspapers and journalists who write for them are always tactful, even when reporting on grisly murders full of gruesome details. I kept the newspaper around, even as it yellowed and the ink smudged from multiple handling and re-reading. Each time I perused it, I always added my own inventions to the text: "When the police discovered Dr. Brown, they thought he was still alive. Turned out the rodents had gotten underneath him and were rattling his corpse back and forth. According to the lone survivor, a kidnapped underage girl held there against her will, Dr. Brown, had a sway about him when he was still alive."

But I am getting ahead of myself. Let us return to the story at hand:

The room I was staying in did nothing to alter my first impressions of the abbey. A bare-minimum airtight compartment with no proper circulation system installed, smelling disgustingly of hydrogen peroxide.

I also had to face the fact that I did not have storage for all the clothes compressed in my over-brimming suitcase—which was about to detonate, sending cotton, polyester and silk articles in every direction.

What the room did have was a wardrobe, though it lacked a mirror on the inside of the door, whether by the age of the design (it looked antique) or by the fact it failed to meet safety standards and regulations, branded as a weapon that patients could use to harm others or themselves once they have shattered the mirror and extracted their preferred piece from the heap. What a strange sight it must be to see your own face, have it imprinted on your consciousness right before you tatter through some ligaments.

Thankfully, there is always a solution, as long as you stay a few steps ahead of your captors. A window at dusk could alternate as my personal mirror; outside of a slightly askew reflection, it was better than nothing.

Minus the aforementioned bed (or have I not mentioned it? it was a bed; it housed a double mattress with railings on each side), there was also a closet—just don't delude yourself into thinking that it was one of those spacious walk-ins every teenage girl dreams of. It was small. The hangers were plastic (God forbid they would have wire hangers you can untwist and jab into your jugular or wherever else) and suspended from an aluminum crosspiece, which was screwed into the wall.

I guess if you were looking for a place to withdraw in splendorous seclusion, this was it.

Does a premeditated act against yourself make you the victim or the culprit responsible for your own demise?

This great mental debate was going on as a pair of orderlies, only two hours into my stay, forcibly strapped down my still sore wrists. I cannot justify my actions; I had lost control, and instead of sharing remembrances of the damaging episodes that contributed to my present breakdown, I shared the contents of my late breakfast (a glass of orange juice and an English muffin) with Dr. Brown.

So, I could not really blame those orderlies

with their bulging muscles, and their immaculate white uniforms for the carelessness and inhumanity they displayed toward me. This was simply their job.

How else do you deal with regurgitation and hysteria, except with containment and sedation? It was time for the two red pills. I was not too sure what they contained, and I am not too sure now, but I swallowed them under the watchful eye of Dr. Brown.

He stuck around afterward, the last time I would see him. Perhaps I was the last person he saw except, of course, for his killer(s). Lacking clairvoyant abilities, sadly, he simply went about his duties, remaining close, monitoring the effects of the therapeutically-friendly medicine as it calmed what he probably classified in his jotted-down notes as an exhibition of maniacal tendencies.

Every two to four hours, Dr. Brown would good-humoredly signal the second of the two orderlies—after the first one had given me my soon-to-be daily intake of pills and a glass of water to wash them down with—over to my bed-ridden side. The second orderly's finger, encased in a skin-tight latex glove containing baby powder on the inside, would slither bulgingly over my gums, moving down the upper and lower levels of the gumline. He would then ask me to "open wide" in a mechanized voice, one lacking any room for empathy, while shining a thin narrow flashlight down my throat.

When all three parties were satisfied with the digestion of the medication, they left me alone to rest. To them, I may have seemed in stable condition, but in reality I perceived myself as an object, an inanimate object, a hollow revolving cylinder undergoing imminent changes due in-part to rising atmospheric pressure while hopped up on god knows what, fading to coma-like sleep and becoming more and more inaccessible to any further rational thinking.

*

For the rest of that night, and partly the next day, I was heavily sedated. I awoke when the medication finally become more and more ineffectual. I staggered out of bed and tried to focus as I approached the only window in my room, which gave a view of the courtyard.

Staggering to that window felt like the most physically strenuous activity I had done in weeks. Through vertical bars blocking the window, reminding me of my imprisonment, I explored the blurry terrain courtesy of my still adjusting eyes.

The courtyard was empty and unpatrolled but had unmistakably undergone certain changes. Additional "enhancements" were added, retrofitting the empty space with the latest in precautionary measures. The cameras and razor-wire fencing made me think of the time I visited Guantánamo Bay where my stepfather had some shadowy business to conduct involving Pentagon defense contracts (his twisted idea of some sort of father-daughter bonding trip).

A firm knock at the door brought me back, but before I could utter a sound, the stranger barged inside and swept my right hand into his own. After a few brief pumps of a handshake—in the process of which the stranger scrutinized my sutured wrists—he finally introduced himself as Dr. Murray and elaborated on the details of being Dr. Brown's replacement.

He was robust, full of manly vigor. He was someone who took great personal risks in his self-less quest to get to the root of the problem, the nitty-gritty responsible for the distortion of the human psyche. He was not one to just gloss over the problem. No not at all. But the type to make an emotional investment while collaborating with you every step of the way. He absolutely abhorred the much-favored principles and techniques! Instead, he chose diversification and experimen-tation thus allowing himself to venture into the great depths of the unknown.

Apparently this was how his patients described him, and he decided to quote them. To me, he seemed like a double-faced well-bred hack from an upper-class family, polished to perfection on the outside and perhaps a bit vulgar somewhere deep down. He didn't exactly exude trustworthiness, especially when I had the privilege to sit in the shorter, non-adjustable chair (by comparison to his black leather, pneumatically-operated throne, which was better suited for a corporate executive than someone with a degree in medicine, and which gave him a clear advantage of elevated positioning as his highness looked down on my ignoble self during our initial get-to-know-one-another session).

He was off to a bad start.

"Why did you do it?"

"You waste no time getting to the point. Well... I have really high standards of myself..."

"No offense, but you cannot be serious about having high standards, especially when you tried to commit suicide."

"I was holding in over three months of depression, and that's how it came out. Aren't you supposed to encourage my progress for not attempting it again instead of criticizing me for something that's behind me now?"

"Is it behind you? Or is the real reason related to the constant supervision and monitoring you have been receiving lately? It is almost like being back home, is it not? Pampered like a child. Let me tell you something. You are not really serious about ending your life with a halfway-open bathroom door and your older sister standing six feet away."

"*Step*sister! And are you calling my actions premeditated?"

"I read your file carefully; you are the perfect student. In your mom's eyes, you are still her little girl, the neat and perfect over-achieving angel that would never willingly inflict pain on herself."

"But I did. I indulged selfishly."

"You planned with care and carefully calculated what the end results would be. Fitted everything perfectly to your needs and ulterior motives, and all just so you could draw your mother's attention to yourself. A giant cry for help. I mean, she was obviously too busy with your other two sisters slash sibling rivals, which can be such a scary thing. But there is a reason why she focused on them; they are her husband's children, who she was trying to welcome to the family, especially when one had a drug addiction and the other was not exactly good at picking her suitors."

"Look, maybe to some extent I reviewed my actions before I executed them. But when I found myself on that cold ceramic tile floor, moments before I passed out, I realized my life could be so much more."

"That is the difference between those who do not fear death, and those who are frightened of death and make a half-hearted attempt in order to draw attention to themselves. Even that insight you just mentioned is not authentic because the experience was not genuine."

"Are you accusing me of fabrication?"

"I am. What I need you to understand is there is nothing wrong with the concept of a blended family. And furthermore, your little attention-seeking stunt was not really about your mother, vying for her attention. No, it hardly had anything to do with her. It is silly. You are a charming young woman exuding femininity yet fretting over courtship to an unhealthy degree, resulting in all this mess." His clinician head turned left, then right, disapprovingly.

"Why are you assuming it was over a guy?"

"Well, was it not?"

"Maybe... but considering my own mother knows nothing about my relationship history, I doubt you got this information from my file."

"You are quite right. I got this piece of much-needed-to-be-documented knowledge from the confines of your mind using a quite common technique known as... assumption."

"Assumptions can get you in a lot of trouble, Doc, especially with a Ph.D. plaque on the wall of your office certifying you as a man of clinically-proven methods, not just fortune teller predictions."

"You will have a chance to sue me for mal-practice once I release you. Now, tell me what happened."

"That night, he came over... and said a couple of things that hit me really hard. When he left, I fell apart; like completely apart and then..."

"...and then?"

"And then, something happened that's too early to talk about."

"I really think you should talk about this."

"And I respect that, but I am hard-headed and stubborn. So, for someone to penetrate that with a sentence starting with, 'I really think,' is just not going to do it for me."

"Let us try a different approach."

"Let's not. This is something best saved for another time. A time when we have gotten to know one another a bit better..."

"At least tell me if his rejection was the last straw, the incident that pushed you over the edge. Perhaps you are just afraid to admit I am right?"

"You aren't entirely wrong, but you aren't

entirely right either. I need more time, that's all."

Of course, I was severely lying through my teeth. This was it, and he nailed it. There were no additional details, nothing to expound on, nothing else to add, but he was really beginning to agitate me.

And I was not under any oath, nor was this the courtroom scene I had to repeatedly face during my parents' ongoing custody battle, so it was quite all right in my mind that I was being irreverent to God, the good doctor, and the policies at large. He did not have to know any of this, this glorified counselor with his bulky frame, breathing hard and watching me like a hawk with his telescope-lens eyeballs. Not everything I said was inaccurate. He just had to wait and see.

To de-stress, I walked out into the courtyard. The sunlight was brilliant, each ray piercing with warmth. Stealing even a glimpse of the sun caused blotches of discoloration within my eyes, and I had to obliterate the out-bursting heavenly light by closing my eyelids. For the past twenty hours, perhaps twenty-five hours, I realized, I had not been myself, stalling, low on fuel, walking zombified from the track marks on my arms, those prickling violent injections with lengthy needles.

Let us not even mention the pills I had to swallow. But basking in this sunlight, smelling the surrounding vegetation (which only existed in the courtyard), walking up to a tree and breaking off a piece of bark to reveal the sap underneath which I applied like a rehabilitative balsamic ointment to my scarred wrists, made me think; really think.

When I walked back to my room, I realized how spick-and-span everything looked. Everything was so idyllic, missing that daily accumulation of dust. A germaphobe with a dustpan would find neither hide nor hair. The room was spotless, but dust just does not evaporate into non-existence.

At the next conversational therapy session, I brought this to Dr. Murray's attention, "Why was my room searched?"

"I guess they did not do a professional job after all."

"You didn't expect a bunch of amateurs to thoroughly go through a girl's private belongings without leaving a trace, did you? Tell them next time to not leave it tidier than they found it. A dead giveaway!"

"It is interesting you identify yourself as a 'girl' instead of a young woman. Very interesting."

"How about answering my question? I had the courtesy to answer yours."

"I fully expected to get away with it. I did not think you would catch on."

"Takes time to open up; remember that, doctor. Don't delay the progress with missteps like this. I thought your kind had the patience of saints."

"We usually reserve that for the clergymen."

"What were you looking for, anyway? Anything specific?"

"We just wanted to make sure you did not

possess something you could intentionally harm yourself with. That is why we are always watching you."

"You watch me?"

"Are you being facetious, Michelle? You perfectly well know we do. Even when you went for your walk in the courtyard, we were right beside you. Perhaps you did not see us, but I know you sensed us whether you want to admit this or not. You happen to be a very clever girl, Michelle."

"Young woman, Doc."

"That is correct. A young woman who always looks before she takes a step; a step we usually try to anticipate to our best abilities."

"Are all patients privileged to this tasteless treatment? Wait. Why haven't I seen anyone else here?"

"Because there is no one else here, Michelle. This facility is on the brink of being demolished; the land will pass hands to the highest bidder and end up being used for the construction of gleaming condominiums. There is just you and me and many unanswered questions that need filling in." He took a moment to subdue his bursting laughter. "You have a schedule, Michelle. That is why you do not see anyone out in the yard."

"Does everyone?"

"No. They are monitored as a large group with low risk of relapsing. They undergo group therapy and act as sponsors for one another. This reliance on each other is a key component in their rehabilitation process."

"And I am seen as high risk? Potential relapse on the horizon?"

"I hope not, but I do not want to rule it out. It is too early to tell."

"Just great. So, we wait."

"You are in safe hands here, Michelle. Nothing bad will happen to you. A relapse is not always physical, the body's response is just the aftermath which may or may not happen. The idea here is to stop your train of thought once it enters this territory of immeasurable anguish. That is your hideaway from the world where you get to re-enact all your pain up on a stage. You turn into a tragedian."

"Tragedian…"

"This is your safety zone. You isolate yourself there. Playing at being an escapologist, not realizing you cannot escape from a life of disharmony by simply outrunning your problems, locking yourself behind the door of a make-believe world which is just as unbalanced as the one you are trying to leave behind. These delusional fantasies claim so many lost individuals every year, all those poor souls with symptoms not too dissimilar from yours. The deflating confidence, engulfing depression, inability to face reality which unfortunately results in senseless death… in certain extreme cases."

"Thanks for making me feel special, Doc. I'm glad to know there's absolutely nothing different about me. Nothing at all that would make me stand out at the Suicidal Thoughts Convention. Just part of the crowd."

"Michelle, you stand out because you are

alive. You happen to be one of the lucky ones. You have a second lease on life. Be grateful you never fully committed to carrying out what the voices in your head were telling you to do. You tried, but you did not adhere to the rules, follow those rules to the letter. You slit across and not down. Just think, once you are better, you can go back home to your loving parents. Your father's campaign will be over by then, and you can enjoy a little less media attention and settle in."

"How do you know about my stepfather's political career?"

"Why would I not know about it?"

"Because my politically-ambitious stepfather would never allow someone like you—a psychologist treating his suicidal stepdaughter—to have knowledge of his identity. He would use a proxy. Which does tie up a couple of loose ends, doesn't it? This leads me to conclude that you are that proxy, high up on his payroll, that slithering snake, a surrogate for someone else's dirty work, presiding over a simulated sanitorium, and once the drug regimen makes me pretty much vegetative, I will continue my stay here indefinitely with occasional visits from my unenlightened mother. Just great."

"Michelle, you know this is not true. This saddens me terribly. You are succumbing to wayward thinking bordering on the delusional."

"The theatricality of your gestures, Doc! We need applause for this riveting performance. Someone throw a bouquet at this man's feet."

I had caught him with his arm up to the elbow in the campaign funds cookie jar. He just sat there speechless and seething, allowing emotions to tongue-tie him in the middle of a meaningful conversation. That was even sloppier than the job his men did on my room.

Before they brought me here, my mother visited me in the hospital. It was a brief visit. The circumstance was morbid, the conversation forced. She was visibly vulnerable and heartbroken, hardly able to speak, but when she spoke at last, she alluded to the fact that I was putting a lot of *unnecessary pressure* on the family, that if one reporter caught wind of a *slip-up* like this, the reportage could cost my stepfather his *entire campaign*.

My stepfather. A man who spent his entire life weighing the odds. He could spot risk a mile away.

I was the high probability risk factor. This place was the deterrent.

For the next couple of days, things returned to normal. Well, almost normal. Outside of the usual-day-to-day routine, I had noticed a change during my regular rounds of depthless conversations with the conniver. Dr. Murray was far more reserved than usual. Less pushy and demanding. A man preoccupied.

Something had changed. I kept imagining a man dynamically descending a set of steep stairs, who suddenly stops. I wanted to know the reason behind this.

I had dislodged something. The truth can be as entrapping as it can be purifying. I looked on with stupefaction, knowing full well that I had hit the nail on the head. And that is when I knew. It *was* just me locked up with Dr. Murray and his strongmen lackeys in this menagerie, watched around the clock by one man (a man watching from the shadows, wrapped securely in his political cloak). Snared, surveilled, and shot on a closed-circuit camera system.

This man. This symbol that refuses to be overthrown.

A man with a brand-new family, a cottage in the Hamptons and a lavish condo on the Upper East Side. Yes, someone who always takes such careful precautions would never allow anyone to publicize his stepdaughter's mental breakdown and attempted suicide in the midst of his crusade for prominence. Not after waging war in the name of his campaign, the battlefield ashen with the charred corpses of his enemies. A man who had always managed any-and-all breaches would not just stand down or sit around idle and irresolute. All I could do was wait.

More days went by, the typical relentlessness of time without pause. The installation of a television set helped, although my allowance only extended to channels that broadcast updates on my stepfather's campaign.

As much as I hated him, he fought zealously to the point of almost being the likable underdog. That magnetizing snakelike smile greeted me every single day. I could not escape it. His voice reverberating inside my head, cuttingly chipping away at what was once impenetrable. Breaking me down, making me more malleable. It was all a little unsettling.

Then came the day I knew it was all over. He was going to lose the campaign. The public finally saw through his trickery, and that is also when I knew it was all over for me. My stepfather was a rabid dog backed into a corner. He had no way out and only one option.

With the current deterioration he was facing, the fickle public with its waning interest, he needed a dramatic turnaround, drastic measures taken to turn the tides of public opinion allowing him to continue his odyssey.

So, I had to die. The showman that he is, I knew he would turn my demise to pure spectacle. Milk it for all it is worth. Want another cliché? He would rise like a phoenix from the ashes to reclaim his spot at the top. A guaranteed victory. I kept probing, trying on other scenarios to see if they fit, teetering between this and that and the other. But I returned every single time. This idea eradicated every other possibility.

After all, here was a savior to a single divorced mother with a teenage child in tow. He opened his arms, he opened his home, he made us a part of his church and hugged us tightly in every photograph. The ideal husband, father, and future leader. The public would see the loss in his face, feel his pain and their own guilt would rise up for betraying him, sleeping with the enemy, favoring his political opponent. At this point he would try to extricate himself from the race until the fickle public would rush back to his side with their bombardment of overwhelming pleas, asking him to stay and not throw in the towel. Sympathy would pour in like a waterfall. The bamboozled public would never turn on him again. And my televised funeral would mark the finale, his coup de grâce. Standing at the podium making a memorable speech, revealing just the right amount of details about my demise, this modest, reserved and much revered public figure would break down just enough to share the cause of the misfortunes that befell his stepdaughter. The maladjustment, slipping grades, skirmishes, substance abuse and attempted suicide, eventually ending up in a treatment facility he paid for until one night she could not handle it anymore and took her own life, shattering the family forever.

And if this was truly his plan all along, the devil's grand design, why the charade with these daily psychiatric sessions, all these painstaking measures taken to mimic an operational facility? Evidence. It had to be that. They were gathering camera footage and documenting my every thought, proof that would support his theories behind my depression and demise. I was unknowingly contributing to my own suicide note. The real note was probably already stashed somewhere for safekeeping, forged in my hand, and written on paper bearing the facility's logo, making it so much more official and final.

This cannot be it... this cannot be how it all ends. I was paranoid. Delusional. It was too absurd. I allowed a smidgen of fear to expand and consume everything. Dr. Murray was here to help. He was here to help me. A clinician with a doctorate's degree. How absurd to think I am alive only because the good doctor thought I still had something important to share.

Around this time, I started to drift off to

sleep, repeating a kind of mantra to myself, *This won't be my resting place...*

As I lay in bed that night (as video-playback would later reveal) Dr. Murray invaded the sanctity of my room. He stood over me for a long time. Watching me. I could not see it from the slightly grainy footage, but I am sure there was a glimmer in his eyes. A horrid glimmer. I have seen it and felt it before. Soulless eyes dispersing infernal light across the vulnerable terrain of my body. Scorching my flesh with his obvious craving. Watching the footage sent shivers down my back.

"It is time, Michelle. I am going to discharge you tonight."

I do not think he cared one way or another if I was awake for what was to come, but I opened my eyes and met his gaze. In the dim light our eyes locked. There was a fixedness in his stare. A steeliness of nerves. He was not preparing himself; he had already reached that stage. His breathing was steady, his voice raspy, like tires skidding on gravel.

"Try not to resist. It will all be over quickly. The more you fight me, the more inclined I will be to use excruciatingly slow and less humane methods. I was about to say try not to scream, or beg for your life, but...

"I guess you could not even if you wanted to with a pillow smothering your face."

He chuckled with no self reproach over his own comment, while I recoiled from his words, unfortunately not fast enough, giving him time to swipe a pillow from under my head and with the debauched swiftness of Marquis De Sade pouncing on his latest conquest, press it firmly over my face.

A methodical killer, he never worried about what he was doing; there was no pivot once he took the first step, and he was pitiless to my pleas as he surely was to all his stifled victims immured to their beds.

"Nothing says affirmation more than asphyxiation," he said as I struggled violently under his strong arms. I needed air, but there was absolutely nothing to gulp at. The air was not there; there was absolutely nothing there.

Just when he overpowered my will to fight and I could not grapple any longer...; just when I was steadfastly becoming immovable; he spoke these words, "I am sure like most people you have wondered at some point about the end. At least now you know."

He kept talking. He would not let me die in peace, serving double duty as an executioner and keynote speaker at my funeral. I relinquished myself to him. He was right. It's not uncommon to wonder how your life will end. And now I knew. I had the golden ticket. The front row seats to a motion picture. I tilted my head back as the parting words to my short-lived life loomed up like credits on that big screen.

But the architecture of that simulated world collapsed, bringing me back, telling me that even a fabricated reality does not last forever, that just

like in real life there is no permanence to anything; that even the actions of my executioner
were transient.

Once the conductor of this torture orchestra
reached optimal satisfaction, he slackened his grip
on the pillow and I started to lose consciousness,
staring uncomprehendingly at his expressionless
face.

When I regained awareness, I tasted an acidic res-
idue from painkillers I did not recall ingesting. I
tried hard to focus my eyes, but the lights in the
room were blinding. Here I was coming out of my
stupor, pumped full of drugs and still somehow
defyingly alive.

Each blink attested to my suspicion of still
being inside the "abbey." Yet it did not seem to
matter just then, for I felt a seismic sensation
against my body like no other. I was part of this
kinetic energy, feeling the force of it, the slightest
fluctuations of the rippling pattern.

I felt embraced from all sides by a warmth, this soothing balm inducing pleasure and disentangling the knots in my muscles. I surrendered, letting go of all past events, permitting the bathtub I did not quite consciously realize I was in to engulf me.

Then I heard his unmistakable voice.

"You know I look at murder-for-hire jobs with the utmost gravity. Client satisfaction is always at the forefront of how I manage my business, with unprecedented success rates to show for it. Just a few small rules to follow: Never break a contract once accepted and always deliver on time. And it comes with a non-monetary bonus. Torture. Which is apart from the rest and never contractually stipulated by my clients. It is a freebie and as long as I do not leave too many marks everyone wins. Oh, how I do enjoy it. *Tremendously* as you will soon see. I admit some may call it an inner flaw. But I digress."

Dr. Murray became the point of convergence for my now refocused eyes. What I wanted to say was the following, "I call it completely unre-markable. That an individual hired to murder someone might actually enjoy it. It's a pairing concept that has been around since Abel slayed his own brother. And my religious teachings are quite rudimentary, I might add. It doesn't matter how sizable the pleasure is, Doc, it's still a part of the overall equation and therefore your speech is quite typical, been-there-done-that and you will find yourself left behind through the sands of time as some ordinary guy aiding crooked pol-iticians and getting your jollies by torturing your teenage targets. You are not abstruse. Not special or complex in any way. Like I said before, or if I haven't I will say it now: Typical and extremely forgetful." An Academy Award-worthy speech. Unfortunately, no sound waves were detectable. My mouth remained stitched shut. There is a time and place for eloquent speeches. Coming out of a drug-induced sleep, tongue-tied and dealing with cottonmouth could be a strong contender for the most terrible timing imaginable.

Dr. Murray's face remained unchanged; this was a man impervious to awkward pauses in the conversation and he did not care if I replied. His only movement was to moisten his lips with his reptilian tongue. I thought he was gathering his thoughts, using the interim to collect himself before he spoke again, except he never did, never felt the need to continue our conversation since it was the only thing delaying him from whatever it was he wanted to do to me involving this tub, now that he had interpolated me in it and filled it with a warm rejuvenating liquid that made me care-free about whether or not I had the miraculous fortune to live another day. The liquid seduced me with its power, pacifying and assuring me that everything was all right, as long as I stayed submerged in it. But now it started to heat up, the water becoming worryingly hot.

Dr. Murray's interest piqued when he noticed my discomfort. He was obviously a man who fervently believed in pain, and he had me right where he wanted me. I was the sole audience to his dissertation on torture techniques. A sad state of affairs for poor little me.

Exercising some of that god-like power, he increased the pressure on the hot water taps. Intolerable pain shot through me. I felt nauseated by the enormity of it. Pain with a sole aim. To triumph. Even through the stupor I pushed, struggled to get out, but Dr Murry's friendly hand on my shoulder kept me down, allowing pain to continue its expansion across my body. To come this far, having faced numerous vicissitudes in my life to end up here being boiled alive.

But not today. I fiercely strived to live, no matter how cruel the world seemed just then, no matter how imbecilic and animalistic were the human actions displayed to me just then, and how mistreated I felt. I found life to be something I wanted, something I desired. I could not allow this pitiless death merchant to blot me out from existence against my will.

The room filled with vapor, with globules of condensation running down the tiled walls next to my head (my only body part jutting above the water) as screams escaped my chimney-like throat. My heart thumped loudly and irregularly; my skin had an epidemic of reddening blisters. And even through all the mistiness, no steam-generated disguise could hide Dr. Murray's sneering expression. This evil creature, this overseer, handler and torturer leering with anticipation for me to die.

And then it happened. My saving grace came in the form of a droplet of sweat which dripped down and made its way into his eyes. I pounced, intercepting this opportunity, disallowing it to slip away while I was still able-bodied to use it.

I pushed Dr. Murray aside, pushed through the overhanging mushroom cloud of steam and made my way out of the room, away from him, away from his homemade torture chamber, leaving a trail of blood in my wake from my still healing wrists which I had reopened with my nails. It was not more than a trickle of blood, but just the right amount to get his attention and lead him straight to me and to my room. But first I had to find my way there through a series of labyrinthine hallways with their seemingly identical levels and doors. Not surprisingly, I never encountered a single soul along the way (more of the good doctor's purported lies exposed).

After some wandering and searching, I finally stumbled across my all-too-familiar containment chamber, ironically happy to be back inside that cell, smiling like a crazed lunatic while darting my eyes all around until I paused on what I had been looking for all along: my bed. I approached it like a madwoman, quickly rearranging the sheets, strategically positioning my pillow, a blanket fort for my personal body double.

I then headed straightaway for the small closet (even smaller since cramping it with my clothes), scavenging and prospecting for weapons.

There I found all that I needed. The cross-piece which I pried from the wall easily enough, and a couple of scarves to patch up my wrists. Lastly, all I had to do was contort my body, bending in half like a gymnast to fit inside, cutting it extremely close as a shaft of light pierced through the darkness of the room.

I watched with bated breath through the narrow slats in the door. The gap widened allowing the intruder to slip inside. He moved around with sufficient care, a sense of purpose. He guided himself across the room noiselessly, always remaining observant of his surroundings, slowly and cautiously working his way toward the pillow placed under the bedsheets. A young girl in hiding.

I solidified my grip on the crosspiece. I was clearheaded, ready to unleash, to pour in all the anger I felt—for my stepfather, this sanatorium, Dr. Murray, and his steamy purgatory.

He removed the blanket and before he could react I braced myself and rushed forward letting out a great bellow, swinging the crosspiece like a baseball bat, trying with all my might to break through the obstruction that was Dr. Murray.

The damage landed squarely on his forehead. I wish I had heard an explosive sound, an excruciating cranial crunch after the hit, one with enough brute force to have left a bloody gaping hole that no staples or stitches or even the best Beverly Hills plastic surgeon specializing in scar revision could ever cure. But I did not have it in me. I was not a murderess. I also was not that strong. So, Dr. Murray, while confused and concussed, was very much alive when I tied him with scarves to the frame of my bed.

Before taking leave of him, I could not restrain myself from giving him a little farewell speech. "You embroil yourself with a high-ranking government official, prostitute yourself for blood money. That's a tough one to extricate yourself from. This man is used to getting what he paid for. He expects results, not colossal failure. There's absolutely no need for me to do anything else here. No need for you to beg for your life. You are as good as dead, Doc. On that note. I think we are done, finished with the treatment, the reforming, I am now going to discharge myself. Goodnight, Dr. Murray. Sleep well."

The rest, my dears, is a happy ending. I not only got away in Dr. Murray's prized possession, his '72 Corvette parked out back, but lived to tell this fascinating tale. The scandalous aftermath was for the news anchors to report, no shortage of sensationalism there. I never did get to sue Dr. Murray for malpractice; he simply vanished. And while there were no bank accounts over-brimming with cash in my real name, or under an assumed identity in Switzerland, I found a decent amount of cash in Dr. Murray's office. Money I was sure came from my stepfather as collateral for a job Dr. Murray accepted and failed to deliver on time which most likely resulted in his death. It was more than enough to get me started on my new journey. Far, far away from here.

ABOUT THE AUTHOR

A native of Kyiv, Ukraine, but living in Canada since the age of eleven, Nick Voro discovered literature at an early age, never quite mustering the ability to put an excellent book down. A recent graduate of the Toronto Film School, Nick divides his time between being a full-time parent and a full-time author.

His debut work, *Conversational Therapy: Stories and Plays*, has recently sold over 200 copies and is part of the library system (United States, Canada, New Zealand, Australia and Scotland).

Lee D. Thompson, an editor and writer from Moncton, New Brunswick, Canada, edited this short story. His books include: a novel in [xxx] dreams from Broken Jaw Press, Mouth Human Must Die from Frog Hollow Press and Apastoral: A Mistopia from Corona/Samizdat. His short fiction has been published in many anthologies, including Random House's Victory Meat, New Fiction from Atlantic Canada and Vagrant Press's The Vagrant Revue of New Fiction. He is the winner of the David Adams Richards Prize (2018) and New Brunswick Book Award (2022). He is the publisher of Galleon Books.